THE Tale OF Hilda Louise

OLIVIER DUNREA

Farrar Straus Giroux

New York

Copyright © 1996 by Olivier Dunrea

All rights reserved

Published simultaneously in Canada by HarperCollins*CanadaLtd*

Color separations by Hong Kong Scanner Arts

Printed in the United States of America by Berryville Graphics

Designed by Lilian Rosenstreich

First edition, 1996

Library of Congress Cataloging-in-Publication Data

Dunrea, Olivier.

The tale of Hilda Louise / Olivier Dunrea. — 1st ed.

p. cm.

[1. Orphans — Fiction. 2. Flight — Fiction. 3. Paris (France) — Fiction.] I. Title.

PZ7.D922Tal 1996 [E] — dc20 95-33511 CIP AC

To Maureen, who once floated in Paris,
and to Ralph and Kristian, who float in Basel

Hilda Louise was an orphan.

When she was very young, her parents disappeared in the Swiss Alps. Her only living relative was her father's younger brother, who could not be found. Hilda Louise was sent to Chez Mes Petits Choux orphanage at 97, rue Saint-Julien-le-Pauvre, Paris.

Hilda Louise lived in a large dormitory with 109 other orphans. She loved her companions, and she loved Madame Zanzibar, but she longed for family of her own. And often she was bored. Nothing exciting or different ever happened. Already she had embroidered 2,357 handkerchiefs.

Then one day, while in the garden, Hilda Louise floated up into the air. Not very high, but far enough off the ground to know that something different was happening at last.

"Mon Dieu!" cried Madame Zanzibar when she saw Hilda Louise.

"Magnifique!" cried the other orphans.

Each day, Hilda Louise floated a little higher. Soon she was able to sit on top of the apple tree growing in the rear garden. From there she looked out over the high brick walls of the orphanage and saw the roofs and balconies of neighboring buildings.

Hilda Louise's newfound talent was useful in capturing flyaway balloons, retrieving balls caught in tree branches, and returning baby birds to the nests from which they had fallen. Floating, Hilda Louise discovered, was marvelous.

Hilda Louise was especially good at polishing high and hard-to-reach places in the Main Hall. Madame Zanzibar often remarked how nice it was to have her help.

In time, Hilda Louise learned to maneuver in the air. She turned somersaults. She soared like a bird, with her arms outstretched. She did death spirals, which made the other orphans gasp and caused Madame Zanzibar to fall in a dead faint.

But what Hilda Louise liked to do most was look out over the brick walls of the orphanage and watch all the activity in the surrounding streets. She saw elegant ladies with large, mysterious packages. She saw children playing with hoops in the cobblestone streets. She saw old men smoking pipes and reading newspapers. She saw romantic couples drinking coffee at sidewalk cafés. All these sights fascinated Hilda Louise, and she wanted to join the people.

One Saturday morning at half past nine, Hilda Louise was sitting on top of the apple tree when a strong gust of wind blew her off the tree and over the walls of the orphanage. "Oh, my!" cried Hilda Louise as she tumbled through the air, head over heels. The wind tossed and turned Hilda Louise; it took her higher and higher.

Hilda Louise saw a rooftop ridgepole and grabbed it to stop herself. She stood on the ridgepole, regaining her composure. She realized she was far away from Chez Mes Petits Choux.

In the street below, a woman was walking a small black dog.

"Bonjour!" Hilda Louise shouted. "Can you tell me how to get back to Chez Mes Petits Choux orphanage?"

The woman looked up and saw a little girl with bright red hair balancing on one foot at the end of a ridgepole. Hilda Louise waved. Then she was carried off by another gust of wind. The woman screamed in alarm. The little black dog barked furiously.

Soon Hilda Louise was floating over what looked like a small forest. She saw wide patches of green grass and a pond with ducks and geese. As she passed the pond, she spied an artist wearing a large straw hat. He was painting a picture.

"Bonjour!" Hilda Louise called to the artist. But the artist did not look up. And before she could say anything more, the wind blew her on her way.

Hilda Louise sighed and floated quietly along.
She discovered that a great number of people were
looking up at her and pointing excitedly. She
glanced over her shoulder at large white clouds.
She did not understand why the people below her
appeared so upset. The clouds were not rain
clouds. "Do not worry!" she shouted to the crowd
below. "It is not going to rain! Those are not rain
clouds!"

The people seemed to be calling to her, but Hilda
Louise could not hear what they were saying.
Then she was swept away again.

Hilda Louise floated past the Eiffel Tower. She waved to the sightseers. But only a small boy saw her and waved back.

Hilda Louise floated to the Arc de Triomphe. She stood for a moment on top of it before being blown away. Then she floated over the spires of the Cathedral of Notre-Dame and made faces at the gargoyles.

At four o'clock in the afternoon, Hilda Louise began to descend from the sky. No matter how hard she tried, she could not rise. She flapped her arms frantically, but she kept falling gently toward the rooftops. She tried doing forward rolls, but still she fell. She dropped past the highest rooftops.

Then Hilda Louise floated through an open garret window and hovered near the ceiling. Below her, painting at an easel, was an artist with bright red hair. Beside him was a large straw hat.

"Bonjour," said Hilda Louise.

The artist looked up. "Mon Dieu!" he cried. He reached up and pulled her to him.

The artist looked hard at Hilda Louise, and Hilda Louise looked hard at him.

"Hilda Louise!" he cried, hugging her tightly to his chest. "At last I have found you!"

"No, Uncle," said Hilda Louise, smiling. "At last *I* have found *you*!"

From then on, Hilda Louise lived happily in her uncle's small garret studio at 124, rue Galande.

She never floated again.

Every Sunday, Hilda Louise and her Uncle Jules visited Madame Zanzibar and the orphans at Chez Mes Petits Choux. Madame Zanzibar served them hot chocolate and strong coffee, cream puffs and chocolate eclairs. It was a special treat for everyone.

"Hilda Louise, my dear," said Madame Zanzibar one Sunday as she poured the hot chocolate. "Did you know that little Marian Lee has begun floating?"

Hilda Louise looked up, and there, near the ceiling, was little Marian Lee, polishing the brass chandelier.

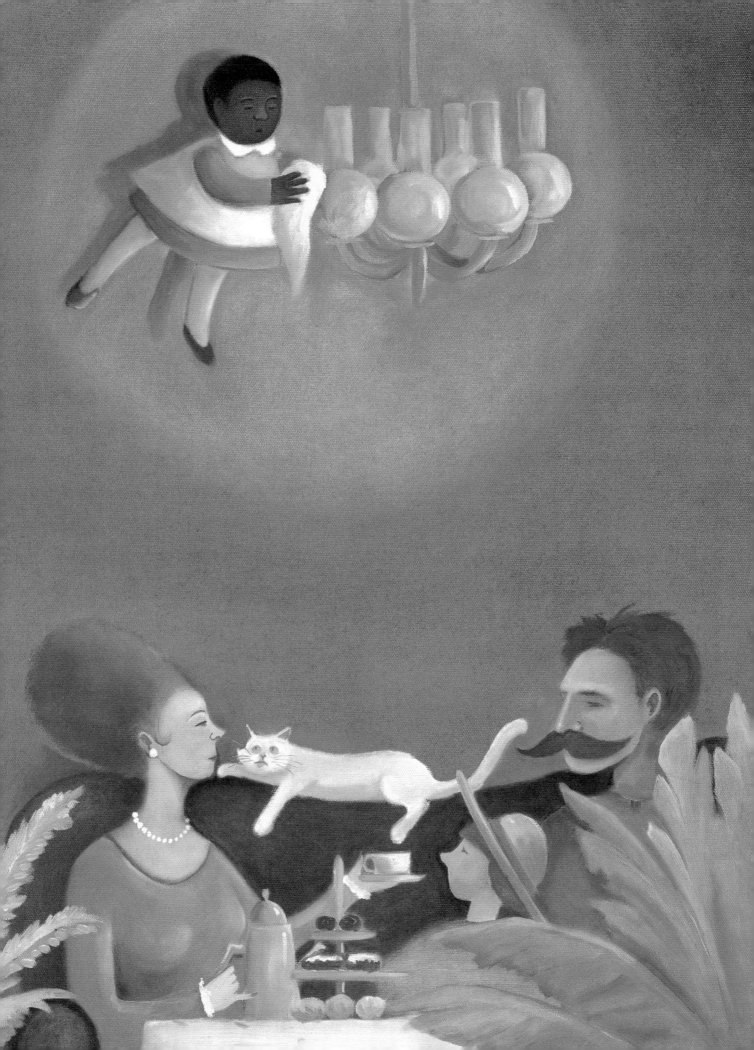